How Can Conservation Save Earth's Resources?

 HOUGHTON MIFFLIN HARCOURT

Printed in Mexico

ISBN: 978-0-544-07353-1

9 10 0908 21 20 19 18 17

4500668768   A B C D E F G

Be an Active Reader!

 Look at these words.

natural resource

renewable resource

nonrenewable
  resource

pollution

conservation

hydroelectric
  energy

geothermal energy

biofuel

 Look for answers to these questions.

What are natural resources?

How do we use resources?

What makes a resource renewable?

What are nonrenewable resources?

What resources do you use at home?

How is pollution harmful?

Why is conservation important?

How does recycling work?

How do reusing and reducing work?

What does "alternative energy" mean?

What are some types of alternative energy?

What energy lies beneath your feet?

How are biological materials used for energy?

What are natural resources?

What's the first natural resource you use in a typical day? Picture yourself getting up in the morning. You take a breath…Stop right there! You're using air, and air is a natural resource, a material found in nature that people can use. You would not be able to live without natural resources. Neither would anyone else, or any other living thing.

Air, water, soil, wind, sunlight, plants, animals, oil, gas, and coal are among the natural resources that we use constantly. Earth is a planet that contains vast resources. But when resources are used by billions of people, some of them can run out.

How many natural resources can you see in this scene? What other resources that you can't see might the people on this farm use?

How do we use resources?

The photo of the farm on page 3 shows these resources:
- the sun, which provides energy for life
- water in the lake for people and animals to drink
- soil, which nourishes plants
- plants, which feed people and animals

Other resources that might be used on a farm include gas for cooking and wood for buildings, fences, and furniture. Minerals in building materials and electronic equipment and metals in vehicles are also natural resources.

Many natural resources are needed in the manufacture of things we use. For example, plastics are not a natural resource, but they're often made from a natural resource, petroleum (oil).

Cars are made mostly of metal, plastic, glass, and rubber. Metal and rubber are natural resources. Plastic and glass are produced using natural resources.

Cutting trees is the beginning of the process of making paper, a long process that requires resources every step of the way.

Are you convinced yet that natural resources are important? Here's another example: paper. Paper is made from wood. To make all the paper that's used in the world, millions of trees are cut down.

But making paper also involves many energy resources. The electric saws that cut the trees are made of metal, and they use electrical energy. The logs are shipped to paper mills by trucks, which use gasoline. The mills use electrical energy to turn the wood into pulp and then into paper. The paper travels to warehouses and stores by truck and train over long distances. These vehicles use gasoline, diesel, and other energy sources. Warehouses and stores use electricity for light, heat, and air conditioning. Energy resources were also used to make every vehicle, building, and piece of equipment.

Earth will run out of sunlight, but not for billions of years. From the human point of view, it will always be here for us, so it is renewable.

What makes a resource renewable?

There are two major types of natural resources: renewable and nonrenewable resources. A renewable resource is one that can be replaced within a reasonable amount of time so that people can continue using it. Renewable resources won't run out—if they are used properly.

Many people take for granted that natural resources will always be there. That's true for some resources, but not all. The biggest renewable resource doesn't even come from Earth. It's sunlight! In one way or another, the sun provides almost all the energy that life on Earth uses. Because we won't run out of sunlight for billions of years, we can keep using it and using it.

Some of our other most important resources are also renewable, such as water. Although we use a lot of it, water runs back to the sea, evaporates into clouds, and falls again as rain through the water cycle.

Air is a renewable resource, too. We breathe it, and yet it is always there. Wind is also renewable, for wind is simply moving air. Air moves because of changes in temperature, and changes in temperature are caused by the sun. As long as the sun, Earth, and air exist, there will be wind.

Plants and animals raised by humans also are renewable resources. We use them for food, but we raise more to replace the ones we use. Since our food comes from those plants and animals, food is a renewable resource, too.

About $\frac{7}{10}$ of Earth is covered with water. But very little is drinkable fresh water. Most is salt water in the oceans and ice at the poles.

What are nonrenewable resources?

Nonrenewable resources are resources that can't be replaced in a reasonable time after they're used. A resource is nonrenewable when there is only a limited supply of it. Once the supply is gone, it is gone for good.

Many nonrenewable resources are elements that humans take out of the ground by mining. That includes metals such as iron, copper, tin, aluminum, gold, and silver.

Soil is also nonrenewable. New soil is made as rock wears down, but the process is very slow. The soil we have now took thousands of years to develop. Therefore, soil is not renewable in anyone's lifetime.

Without soil, there wouldn't be many plants. Yet we can't renew this resource in a reasonable time.

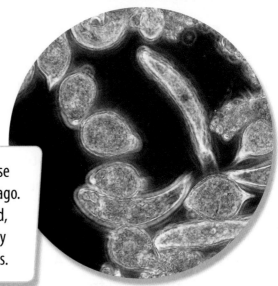

Tiny sea organisms like these also lived millions of years ago. After they died and decayed, natural processes eventually turned them into fossil fuels.

Fossil fuels are extremely important nonrenewable resources. Oil, gas, and coal are the three big fossil fuels. They are the major fuels that people use for transportation, heating, and cooking. Our cars, factories, and homes run on them. Yet these resources will run out someday.

"Fossil" fuels got their name because they come from the bodies of ancient living things. Millions of years ago, animals and plants lived and died. Their bodies decayed. Over time, layers of sediment covered the remains. Heat and pressure turned the decayed material into new materials packed full of energy. Our way of life today depends on materials that took millions of years to make. It would take millions of years to replace them.

What resources do you use at home?

Natural resources are present in every city and every home. If you look in your home for ways you use natural resources, you'll be amazed. Take just one common resource—water. Almost as soon as you get up, you turn on a faucet, wash, and brush your teeth. You drink water throughout the day. You eat food cooked in water. You use a lot more water when you take a shower or bath and when your clothes are washed.

Now look at a computer. A computer uses electricity. Electricity is produced from natural resources such as coal and water. Computer cables contain metals such as copper, as well as rubber and plastic.

Each person in the United States uses 80 to 100 gallons of water a day!

Some of the metals in computers are found in very limited amounts.

Then there are all of the chemical elements needed to make the computer parts. You'll find silicon, of course, and even tiny amounts of gold. Computer parts contain more than 60 elements, some of which are rare. Minerals are mined all over the world to provide these elements.

Everything in the structure of your home—wood, brick, tile, stone—is also a natural resource. The floors, walls, and furniture all came from natural resources. So did all the appliances. You probably have a refrigerator, stove, television, and more. Every one of them contains natural resources and was made using natural resources.

How is pollution harmful?

Using up natural resources is a serious problem the world faces. A related problem is pollution, the damage that using resources does to Earth. Pollution can make air, water, and soil dirty and even dangerous.

The biggest cause of pollution in the air is the burning of fossil fuels. Think about all the cars, trucks, and buses in the world. There are more than a billion of them! Picture a billion vehicles burning gasoline and spewing exhaust into the air. Some of the substances in the exhaust can harm health. Some of them smell bad. They undergo chemical changes in the air that form smog. Energy stations that burn fossil fuels also cause air pollution. So do some factories.

Air pollution can lead to lung disease. Fortunately, some cities in the United States and elsewhere have reduced their air pollution.

As the population increases, the world needs more water. At the same time, water pollution increases.

Water and soil can also become polluted. Some water pollution results from trash dumped into rivers, lakes, and seas. Water pollution also results when chemicals from manufacturing are released from factories into sewers. Even farming can create water pollution. The water that flows across land is called runoff. When runoff picks up farm chemicals that fertilize the soil or kill pests, it spreads the chemicals into rivers and streams and underground.

Runoff can also pollute the soil. Rain runs off roads and parking lots and picks up pollutants. It runs downhill and can ruin the soil of nearby farms when it soaks into the ground. Rain that falls on polluted soil can seep deep under the ground and mix with the water that many cities tap into for their water supply.

Why is conservation important?

Using natural resources creates problems. It's possible to use up resources so quickly that they may not be available in the future. Our harnessing of natural resources often pollutes the environment. There's also the problem of waste. Landfills, places where towns and cities put their trash, grow more numerous—and larger—as the years pass. Where can we *put* all that trash? What can we do with it that makes more sense than just dumping it in a huge pile?

Conservation—the wise use of resources in order to avoid wasting them or harming Earth—is one answer to those problems. There are three major ways to conserve. You can remember them as the 3 Rs: reduce, reuse, and recycle.

Of the 3 Rs, recycling is probably the most familiar to you. Many U.S. communities recycle paper, plastic, and other materials.

How does recycling work?

Recycling is making new things from thrown-away materials. Recycling begins when people put their recyclable trash in bins and trucks pick it up. It continues when recycling centers sort the trash into types, such as metal, glass, paper, and plastic. They then sell those materials to factories that make new products from them.

Recyclable trash items must be sorted before they're sold. A mill that recycles old paper into new paper, for instance, doesn't want metal from old cans mixed in.

There are several types of recyclable plastic. Not every community recycles all of them. Plastic items have little triangles containing numbers from 1 to 7. Each number shows what type of plastic an item is made of.

Plastics 1, 2, and 6 are the most often recycled. Check with your recycling center to find out which types it takes.

How do reusing and reducing work?

Reusing resources means using old items for new purposes. You can do a lot of reusing at home. Reuse old clothes by giving them to others or cutting them into rags. You can reuse an old mug as a pen holder or turn a coffee can into a flower pot.

Reducing is simply using less. To reduce resource use, try some of the following. Take shorter showers. Turn the water off while you brush your teeth. Turn off lights when no one is in a room. Ask to keep your home a couple of degrees cooler in winter and warmer in summer. Walk or ride your bike instead of being driven places. When shopping, bring your own cloth bags instead of using plastic or paper bags from a store.

By keeping cars longer, people can use fewer of Earth's resources.

What does "alternative energy" mean?

So far, you've learned about the most common ways of using Earth's energy resources. People all over the world rely on fossil fuels to get places, make products, cook food, and heat and cool buildings. But because fossil fuels pollute, and because they may run out, people are searching for new sources of energy, this time from renewable resources. Energy produced from renewable resources is known as alternative energy.

Alternative energy isn't going to run out soon. Most forms of alternative energy are "clean," meaning that they don't pollute, or they pollute much less than fossil fuels do.

People have used the energy in running water for thousands of years. Today, we are harnessing the energy of water in new ways.

What are some types of alternative energy?

Important sources of alternative energy are the sun, wind, water, and Earth itself. All of these sources are renewable ones. They will be around as long as people will be.

You may have heard of solar energy. Solar energy is the energy that comes to Earth from the sun. People can capture the sun's energy by using solar cells, small devices that turn light energy into electrical energy. Solar cells are brought together into larger groups to make solar panels. You may have seen these panels on the roofs of some homes or buildings. The electricity from solar panels is used to provide heat and light. Solar energy is free; you don't buy it from an electric company.

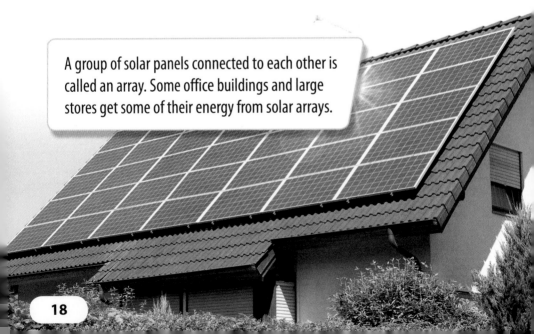

A group of solar panels connected to each other is called an array. Some office buildings and large stores get some of their energy from solar arrays.

Modern wind turbines produce much more energy than old-fashioned windmills.

Using wind energy is an old idea, as old as windmills. Windmills of long ago pumped water. Today's windmills produce electricity and are called wind turbines. Groups of wind turbines are often set up in places where we can count on the wind to blow.

Energy from water, called hydroelectric energy, has been used throughout history. Today, water that flows through dams turns turbines that produce electricity. Another form of hydroelectric energy comes from ocean tides. Tides are completely predictable and can be used as an energy source. Tide water can be moved through turbines. Tidal energy stations can be built in places where the difference between high tide and low tide is 16 meters or more. Those places include parts of the northwestern and northeastern United States.

What energy lies beneath your feet?

One kind of energy that humans draw up from beneath Earth's surface is called geothermal energy. Deep beneath its surface, Earth is hot. Liquid rock heats pools of water several kilometers below, and wells can bring up the hot water and steam. At energy stations, geothermal energy can run electric generators.

Geothermal energy from about a meter underground is also useful. There, the ground stays at about the same temperature in all seasons. It's cooler than the air above ground in summer and warmer than the air in winter. Geothermal heat pumps beneath homes draw heat up in the winter to heat the homes. They pump heat into the soil in summer to cool them.

Large sources of geothermal energy can be found near geysers and hot springs. These are water sources that have been heated below the surface of Earth.

How are biological materials used for energy?

Biofuels are fuels produced by biological materials. Ethanol is a biofuel made from corn. Biodiesel is made from soybean oil.

Scientists are now finding new ways to produce biofuels. One type is being made from a grass called switchgrass. Another is being made from algae, an organism that often covers lakes and ponds. Even cow manure can become biofuel!

Not only is alternative energy good for Earth, it's good for business. For example, old lumber mills and paper mills can be turned into biofuel factories. Wind turbine "farms" can make money from empty land.

The way we use resources in the future may be very different from the way we've used them in the past.

Today, when people see algae clogging a pond, they might say, "Yuck!" In the future, they might say, "There's an energy source!"

Find Air Pollution

Some particles of air pollution are big enough to see. Find places where there might be different amounts of pollution in your community. Gather at least four empty small glass jars and line the insides with petroleum jelly. Place some jars in areas around your home. Place at least one jar outside. Be sure to place all your jars in safe places where they will not be disturbed for one week. Label each jar with its location. After a week, gather all your jars and compare the amounts of dirt that have stuck to the petroleum jelly. Write a report that includes your observations and conclusions.

Write a Letter to the Past

People living a century ago didn't think much about the problems of pollution or about resources running out. Write a letter to your great-great-grandparent explaining these problems and why they're important today. Explain one or more forms of alternative energy.

Glossary

biofuel [BY•oh•FYOOL] A fuel produced by biological materials, such as wood.

conservation [kahn•ser•VAY•shuhn] The process of preserving and protecting an ecosystem or a resource.

geothermal energy [jee•oh•THER•muhl EN•er•jee] A type of energy produced naturally beneath Earth's surface.

hydroelectric energy [hy•droh•ee•LEK•trik EN•er•jee] Energy produced by using the mechanical energy of falling water.

natural resource [NACH•er•uhl REE•sawrs] Anything from nature that people can use.

nonrenewable resource [nahn•rih•NOO•uh•buhl REE•sawrs] A resource that, once used, cannot be replaced in a reasonable amount of time.

pollution [puh·LOO·shuhn] Any waste product or contamination that harms or dirties an ecosystem and harms organisms.

renewable resource [rih·NOO·uh·buhl REE·sawrs] A resource that can be replaced within a reasonable amount of time.